Q q

Quentin's Quiz and the Letter **Q**

Alphabet Friends

by Cynthia Klingel and Robert B. Noyed

The
**Child's
World**®

The Child's World®

**Published in the United States of America
by The Child's World®**
P.O. Box 326
Chanhassen, MN 55317-0326
800-599-READ
www.childsworld.com

The Child's World®: Mary Berendes, Publishing Director

Editorial Directions, Inc.: E. Russell Primm, Editorial
Director; Emily Dolbear, Line Editor; Ruth Martin,
Editorial Assistant; Linda S. Koutris, Photo Researcher
and Selector

Photographs ©: Corbis: Cover & 9; Anderson Ross/
Photodisc/Getty Images: 10; Bohemian Nomad
Picturemakers/Corbis: 13; Don Farrall/Photodisc/Getty
Images: 14; Bob Krist/Corbis: 17; Roman Soumar/
Corbis: 18; C Squared Studios/Photodisc/Getty
Images: 21.

Library of Congress Cataloging-in-Publication Data
Klingel, Cynthia Fitterer.
 Quentin's quiz and the letter Q / by Cynthia Klingel
and Robert B. Noyed.
  p. cm. — (Alphabet readers)
Summary: A simple story about the questions on
Quentin's quiz introduce the letter "q".
 ISBN 1-59296-107-X (Library Bound : alk. paper)
 [1. Questions and answers—Fiction. 2. Alphabet.] I.
Noyed, Robert B. II. Title. III. Series.
 PZ7.K6798Qv 2003
 [E]—dc21   2003006605

Note to parents and educators:

The first skill children acquire before becoming successful readers is individual letter recognition. The Alphabet Friends series has been created with the needs of young learners in mind. Each engaging book begins by showing the difference between the capital letter and the lowercase letter. In each of the books on the vowels and the consonants c and g, children are introduced to the different sounds that the letter can make. Finally, children see that the letters can be found at the beginning of a word, in the middle of a word, and in most cases, at the end of a word.

Following the introduction, children meet their Alphabet Friends. The friend in each story encounters many words that include the featured letter of that book. Each noun that begins with the title letter is highlighted in red with the initial letter of the word in bold. Above the word is a rebus drawing that establishes a strong picture cue.

At the end of each book, we have included three words lists. Can your young learners find all the words in each book with the title letter in them?

Let's learn about the letter **Q.**

The letter **Q** can look like this: **Q.**

The letter **Q** can also look like this: **q.**

The letter **q** can be at the

beginning of a word, like queen.

queen

The letter **q** can be in the

middle of a word, like aquarium.

a**q**uarium

The English language doesn't have

any words that end in **q.**

Quentin is on his way to school. He has to

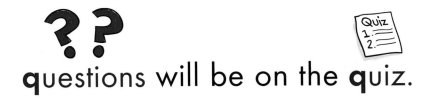

take a **q**uiz today. He wonders what the

questions will be on the **q**uiz.

The teacher gives **Q**uentin the **q**uiz.

The classroom is very quiet. The first

question looks easy. What bird makes

a "quack" sound?

A duck makes a quack sound! Quentin

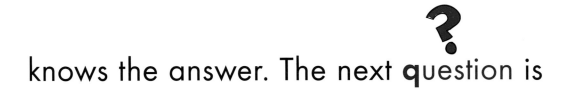knows the answer. The next question is

about math. Which coins add up to a

quarter?

Two dimes and one nickel equal a

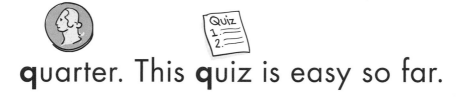

quarter. This **q**uiz is easy so far.

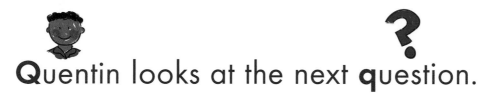

Quentin looks at the next **q**uestion.

What sport does a **q**uarterback play?

A **q**uarterback plays on a football team!

There are only two more **q**uestions on the

quiz. **Q**uentin has known all the answers.

What is a **q**uilt?

A **q**uilt is a colorful cover for a bed.

Quentin was quick to write that

answer. What does a **q**ueen wear on

her head?

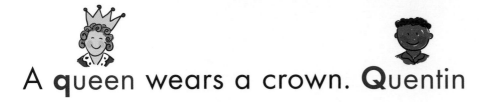

A **q**ueen wears a crown. **Q**uentin

finishes the **q**uiz. It is time to quit. Do you

understand what the **q**uiz was about?

It was about the letter **Q**!

Fun Facts

 The **q**uarter is a U.S. coin worth 25 cents. Since 1932, all quarters have had the head of George Washington on one side. Some **q**uarters have a bald eagle, the national bird of the United States, on the opposite side. Other **q**uarters have a colonial drummer on one side instead of an eagle. There are also **q**uarters that replace the eagle with designs that celebrate each of the 50 U.S. states.

 A **q**ueen is a woman who rules a kingdom, or who is the wife of a king. Kings and **q**ueens rule under a system of government called a monarchy. Under a monarchy, one person has the right to govern for his or her entire life. Usually these people, called monarchs, inherit their positions. That means the position is passed down to them from their mother or father, or sometimes from another family member. Throughout history, there have been many important **q**ueens, including Cleopatra, **q**ueen of Egypt, **Q**ueen Elizabeth I of England, and **Q**ueen Isabella I of Spain.

To Read More

About the Letter Q

Bruckner, Susan B., and L. Kingman. *The Letter Q: Consonant Easy Readers.* Westminster, Calif.: Teacher Created Materials, 1997.

Klingel, Cynthia. *Quack! The Sound of the Letter Q.* Chanhassen, Minn.: The Child's World, 2000.

About Quarters

Holtzman, Caren, and Betsy Day (illustrator). *Quarter from the Tooth Fairy.* New York : Scholastic, 1995.

Williams, Deborah, and Gloria Gedeon (illustrator). *Quarter Story.* Rocky River, Ohio: Kaeden Corporation, 1997.

About Queens

Andreotti, Lindsay, and Julie Hartley (illustrator). *The Queen and the Coffee Bean.* Seattle: Hara Publishing, 2001.

Stanley, Diane, and Peter Vennema. *Cleopatra.* New York: Morrow Junior Books, 1994.

Stanley, Diane, and Peter Vennema. *Good Queen Bess: The Story of Elizabeth I of England.* New York: Four Winds Press, 1990.

Words with Q

Words with **Q** at the Beginning

quack

quarter

quarterback

queen

Quentin

question

questions

quick

quiet

quilt

quit

quiz

Words with **Q** in the Middle

aquarium

equal

About the Authors

Cynthia Klingel has worked as a high school English teacher and an elementary teacher. She is currently the curriculum director for a Minnesota school district. Cynthia Klingel lives with her family in Mankato, Minnesota.

Robert B. Noyed started his career as a newspaper reporter. Since then, he has worked in communications and public relations for a Minnesota school district for more than fourteen years. Robert B. Noyed lives with his family in Brooklyn Center, Minnesota.